A NOTE TO PARENTS

When your children are ready to "step into reading," giving them the right books is as crucial to their development as giving them the right food to eat. **Step into Reading®** books feature exciting stories and information reinforced with lively, colorful illustrations that make learning to read fun, satisfying, and rewarding. We have even taken *extra* steps to keep your child engaged by offering Step into Reading Sticker books, Step into Reading Math books, and Step into Reading Phonics books, in addition to fabulous fiction and nonfiction.

Learning to read, Step by Step:

- **Super Early** books (Preschool–Kindergarten) support pre-reading skills. Parent and child can engage in "see and say" reading using the strong picture cues and the few simple words on each page.
- **Early** books (Preschool–Kindergarten) let emergent readers tackle one or two short sentences of large type per page.
- **Step 1** books (Preschool–Grade 1) have the same easy-to-read type as Early, but with more words per page.
- **Step 2** books (Grades 1–3) offer longer and slightly more difficult text while introducing contractions and clauses. Children are often drawn to our exciting natural science nonfiction titles at this level.
- **Step 3** books (Grades 2–3) present paragraphs, chapters, and fully developed plot lines in fiction and nonfiction.
- **Step 4** books (Grades 2–4) feature thrilling nonfiction illustrated with exciting photographs for independent as well as reluctant readers.

Remember: The grade levels assigned to the six steps are intended only as guides. Some children move through all six steps rapidly; others climb the steps over a period of a few years. Either way, these books will help children "step into reading" for life!

To Mallory, Pat Jensen, and
Maera Bear—
fine ladies all!

Copyright © 2002 by Antonia Zehler
All rights reserved under International and Pan-American Copyright Conventions.
Published in the United States by Random House Children's Books, a division of
Random House, Inc., New York, and simultaneously in Canada by Random House
of Canada Limited, Toronto.

Library of Congress Cataloging-in-Publication Data
Zehler, Antonia.
Two fine ladies : tea for three / by Antonia Zehler.
p. cm. — (Step into reading. Step 1 book)
SUMMARY: Two ladies make friends with a bear and invite him to have tea at their house.
ISBN 0-375-81105-2 (trade) — ISBN 0-375-91105-7 (lib. bdg.)
[1. Friendship—Fiction. 2. Bears—Fiction. 3. Tea—Fiction.] I. Title.
II. Step into reading. Step 1 book.
PZ7.Z36 Twk 2002 [E]—dc21 2002017830

www.randomhouse.com/kids

Printed in the United States of America First Edition 10 9 8 7 6 5 4 3 2 1

STEP INTO READING, RANDOM HOUSE, and the Random House colophon are registered trademarks of
Random House, Inc.

Step into Reading

🌹 Two Fine Ladies 🌹
Tea for Three

A Step 1 Book

by Antonia Zehler

Random House 🏠 New York

One day, two fine ladies
went out for a drive.

They saw a lonely bear
by the side of the road.

They stopped to visit

and became fast friends.

They asked the bear
home for tea.

"You can ride with us,"
they said.

VROOM!

They drove
to the ladies' house.

"Welcome!"

the ladies said.

"Won't you please
come in?"

"You are quite bare,"
said one fine lady.

The two fine ladies
looked in their trunk.

They found something
nice for the bear to wear.

"You look lovely!"
said the ladies.

"Time for tea!"

The bear drank the tea.

The bear ate the cookies.

The bear made a mess!

"Oh no!"

cried the two fine ladies.

"How impolite!"

The bear was sorry.

He took off the jacket.

He wiped up the tea
and the cookie crumbs.

He shook hands
with the ladies

and walked sadly
to the door.

"Wait!" cried the ladies.

"Please don't go!

Polite or not,

you are our friend."

The bear agreed to stay.

The bear and the ladies
finished the tea
and cookies.

Then it was bedtime.

So the ladies brushed
the bear's teeth.

They gave him a bath.

And they tucked him into bed.

Good night.